Alien Invaders

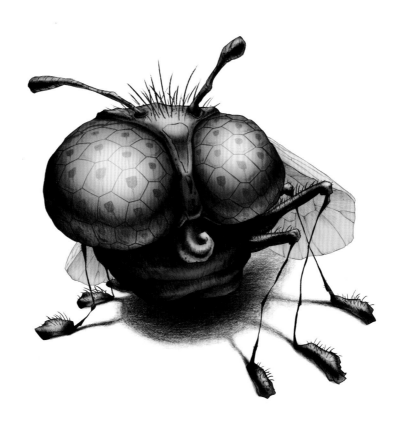

Invasores extraterrestres

Written by Lynn Huggins-Cooper
Illustrated by Bonnie Leick

For Alex, Bethany, Eleanor—
and all the happy hours spent bug hunting!
—Lynn Huggins-Cooper

For my family, my friends, and all the bugs I encountered in my youth.
—Bonnie Leick

Text ©2005 by Lynn Huggins-Cooper
Illustration ©2005 Bonnie Leick
Translation ©2005 Raven Tree Press

Huggins-Cooper, Lynn.

Alien invaders / written by Lynn Huggins-Cooper; illustrated by Bonnie Leick; translated by Cambridge BrickHouse = Invasores extraterrestres / escrito por Lynn Huggins-Cooper; illustrado por Bonnie Leick; traducción al español de Cambridge BrickHouse —1st ed. —McHenry, IL: Raven Tree Press, 2005.

p. ; cm.

SUMMARY: A child compares garden creatures to what he knows of space invaders. Bugs and creepy crawlers abound in far–out illustrations.

Bilingual Edition
ISBN: 978-0-9724973-9-8 hardcover
ISBN: 978-0-9741992-7-6 paperback

English-only Edition
ISBN: 978-1-934960-83-7 hardcover

Audience: pre-K to 3rd grade
Title available in English-only or bilingual English-Spanish editions

1. Insects—Juvenile fiction. 2. Gardens—Juvenile fiction. 3. Imagination—Juvenile fiction.
4. Life on other planets—Juvenile fiction. 5. Bilingual books—English and Spanish.
6. [Spanish language materials—books.] I. Illust. Leick, Bonnie. II. Title.
III. Invasores extraterrestres

LCCN: 2003109087

Printed in Taiwan
10 9 8 7 6 5 4
First Edition

Free activities for this book are available at www.raventreepress.com

Raven Tree Press
A Division of Delta Systems Co., Inc.
www.raventreepress.com

Alien Invaders

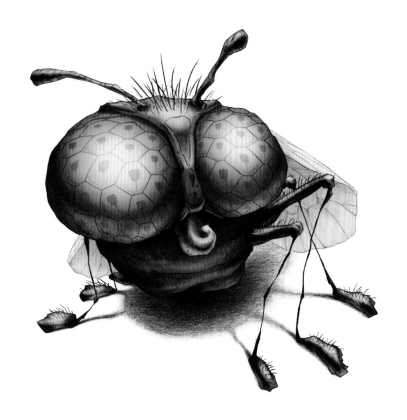

Invasores extraterrestres

Written by Lynn Huggins-Cooper
Illustrated by Bonnie Leick

I heard that aliens are little green men.

Dicen que los extraterrestres son hombrecitos verdes.

Wrong!

The alien invaders are here.

¡Falso!

Los invasores extraterrestres están aquí.

They set up camp
in our garden.

Tienen su campamento
en nuestro jardín.

8

They have robot legs.
They wear shiny
suits and helmets.

Tienen patas de robots.

Usan trajes y cascos brillantes.

They watch us
with camera–lens eyes.
Are they taking pictures?

Nos vigilan con ojos
de lente de cámara.
¿Estarán sacando fotos?

Some fly and dive.

Algunos vuelan y bajan en picada del cielo.

Others slither.
They leave clues.

Otros se deslizan.
Dejan pruebas.

I hear them whisper
in secret languages.
I see them dance
strange dances.

Los escucho susurrar
en idiomas secretos.
Los observo bailar
danzas extrañas.

They build cities under our feet...

Construyen ciudades bajo nuestros pies...

and spin
dangerous traps.

y tejen
trampas peligrosas.

They sneak
into our houses
and watch us.

Entran a hurtadillas

en nuestras casas

y nos vigilan.

There are many more of them than us.

Son mucho más que nosotros.

Mom says they
are just bugs.
But I am making friends
with them, just in case.

Mamá dice que
simplemente son insectos.
Pero me estoy haciendo
amigo de ellos, por si acaso.

They sure look
like aliens to me!

¡A mí sí me
parecen extraterrestres!

Vocabulary  Vocabulario

alien(s)	el (los) extraterrestre(s)
camp(s)	el (los) campamento(s)
garden(s)	el (los) jardín (jardines)
leg(s)	la(s) pata(s)
eye(s)	el (los) ojo(s)
picture(s)	la(s) foto(s)
clue(s)	la(s) prueba(s)
dance(s)	la(s) danza(s)
city / cities	la(s) ciudad(es)
house(s)	la(s) casa(s)
bug(s)	el (los) insecto(s)
friend(s)	el (los) amigo(s)